For Laurence and Michel
    –Q.G.

First published in the United States, Great Britain, Canada, Australia, and New Zealand
in 2010 by North-South Books Inc., an imprint of NordSüd Verlag AG, CH-8005 Zürich, Switzerland.

Distributed in the United States by North-South Books Inc., New York 10001.

Library of Congress Cataloging-in-Publication Data is available.

Printed in Belgium by Proost N.V., B 2300 Turnhout, August 2010.

ISBN: 978-0-7358-2324-2 (trade edition)

1 3 5 7 9 • 10 8 6 4 2

www.northsouth.com

Carlo Collodi

PINOCCHIO

illustrated by
Quentin Gréban

NorthSouth
New York / London

CHAPTER 1

How it happens that Master Cherry, the carpenter, finds a piece of wood that laughs and cries like a child.

Once upon a time, there was . . .

"A king!" my young readers are going to say.

No, children, you are wrong. Once upon a time, there was a piece of wood.

The fact is that one fine day this piece of wood was lying in the shop of an old carpenter named Master Cherry, so named because the end of his nose was always as red and shiny as a ripe cherry.

No sooner had Master Cherry set eyes on the piece of wood than his face beamed with delight. He rubbed his hands together with satisfaction and murmured to himself, "This wood has come at the perfect moment. It is just in time to make the leg of a little table."

Then he picked up a sharp ax. But just as he was poised to give the first stroke, he heard a very small voice. "Don't strike me!"

Imagine the look on good old Master Cherry's face! Terrified, he searched all around the room trying to discover where the little voice could possibly have come from, but he saw nobody.

"I see," he said, laughing and scratching his wig. "That voice, I imagined it. Now back to work."

And taking up the ax, he struck a tremendous blow on the piece of wood.

"Ow! Ow! You have hurt me!" cried the same little doleful voice.

This time Master Cherry was petrified with fear. "Where on earth can that little voice have come from? There is not another living soul here. This piece of wood is like any other piece of wood: fuel for the fire. Unless there is someone hidden inside? If someone is in there, I'll find out, and it will be the worse for him."

He seized the poor piece of wood and began to beat it mercilessly against the wall. Then he stopped to listen for a little lamenting voice. Nothing!

"I see," he said, pushing up his wig and forcing himself to laugh. "Evidently the little voice that said 'Ow! Ow!' was all in my imagination. Now back to work."

Putting aside the ax, he took up his plane; but while he was running it up and down, he heard the same little voice laugh and say, "Stop. You are tickling me."

This time poor Master Cherry felt as if he had been struck by lightning. When at last he opened his eyes, he was sitting on the floor. His face was changed. Even the end of his nose, instead of being crimson as it usually was, had turned blue from fright.

CHAPTER 2

Master Cherry makes a present of the piece of wood to his friend Geppetto, who takes it to make himself a wonderful puppet capable of dancing, fencing, and leaping like an acrobat.

Just at that moment someone knocked on the door.

"Come in," said the carpenter from where he sat on the floor. He hadn't the strength to rise to his feet.

A lively little old man stepped briskly into the shop. His name was Geppetto.

"Good day, Master Antonio," said Geppetto. "What are you doing there on the floor?"

"I am teaching calculus to ants. What has brought you to me, neighbor Geppetto?"

"My legs. Master Antonio, I have come to ask you a favor."

"Here I am, ready to serve you," replied the carpenter, rising to his knees.

"This morning an idea came into my head. I thought I would make a beautiful wooden puppet, a wonderful puppet that would know how to dance, fence, and leap like an acrobat. With this puppet I would travel all over the world to earn a piece of bread and a glass of wine."

"And what can I do to help you?"

"I need wood to make my puppet."

Delighted with this request, Master Antonio hurried to his bench and fetched the piece of wood that had frightened him so much. But just as he was going to give it to his friend, the piece of wood shook and, wriggling forcefully from his hands, struck a hard blow to Geppetto's shins.

"Ah! Is that your courteous way of offering gifts, Master Antonio? You almost lamed me."

"I swear to you, it wasn't me."

"Ah, so it's my fault."

"No, it's the wood's fault."

"I know it was the wood, but you're the one who hit my legs with it."

"I did not hit you with it!"

"Liar!"

Geppetto fell upon the carpenter, and they fought furiously. When the battle was over, Master Antonio had two more scratches on his nose, and Geppetto had two buttons missing from his waistcoat. Their accounts being squared, they shook hands and swore to remain good friends for the rest of their lives.

Geppetto then took his fine piece of wood and, thanking Master Antonio, returned limping to his house.

CHAPTER 3

*Geppetto, having returned home, sets to work on his puppet, which
he names Pinocchio. The first pranks are played by the puppet.*

As soon as he got home, Geppetto took out his tools and set to work to carve the puppet that he had decided to call Pinocchio. First he made the head. Imagine Geppetto's astonishment when he had finished the eyes and saw that they moved, and that they were staring right at him.

Geppetto proceeded to carve the nose, but no sooner had he made it than it began to grow. The more he cut it off to shorten it, the longer the impertinent nose grew!

Geppetto had not even completed the mouth when it began to laugh and make fun of him.

After the mouth, he made the chin, throat, shoulders, stomach, arms, and hands. The hands were hardly finished when Geppetto felt his wig snatched from his head.

"Pinocchio! Give me back my wig instantly!"

But instead of returning it, Pinocchio put it on his own head.

"You rascal! You are not yet finished and already you show such a lack of respect for your father. That is bad, my boy, very bad!" And he blotted a tear.

Only the legs and feet remained to be done. When Geppetto had finished them, he set the puppet on the floor to teach him to walk. Geppetto led him by the hand and showed him how to put one foot before the other. Soon Pinocchio began to walk by himself. Then he ran all around the room and right out the door, where he bounded into the street and took off running. His wooden feet clunked against the pavement, making as much clatter as twenty pairs of peasants' clogs.

"Stop him! Stop him!" shouted Geppetto, running after him.

As luck would have it, a police officer arrived. Bravely planting himself in the middle of the road, he waited to intercept the puppet, caught Pinocchio by the nose, and returned him to Geppetto.

"We will go home at once," Geppetto told Pinocchio, "and as soon as we arrive, we will deal with what you have done."

When Pinocchio heard this, he threw himself on the ground and refused to take another step. In the meantime, idlers and curious people crowded around them. Each had an opinion.

Some said, "Poor puppet, he's right not to wish to go home. Who knows how old Geppetto will treat him?"

And others added meanly, "Geppetto seems all right, but with boys he's a regular tyrant. If that poor puppet is left in his hands, Geppetto will tear it to pieces."

After a great deal of talk, much of it convincing, the police officer set Pinocchio free and led Geppetto to prison.

CHAPTER 4

The story of Pinocchio and the Talking Cricket, from which we see that naughty boys can't stand to be corrected by those who know more than they do.

While Geppetto was being led off to prison, the rascal Pinocchio ran home at top speed. Once there he locked all of the bolts, threw himself on the floor, and sighed in satisfaction. But his satisfaction didn't last long, because somewhere in the room he heard someone saying, "*Cri-cri-cri!*"

"Who's calling me?" asked Pinocchio, frightened.

"It's me!"

Pinocchio turned. An enormous Cricket was crawling slowly up the wall.

"I am the Talking Cricket, and I have lived in this room for more than a hundred years."

"Yeah, but now it's my house," said the puppet, "so get out right now and don't come back."

"I will not leave until I have told you an important truth," said the Cricket.

"Fine, then hurry up and tell me."

"Woe to children who rebel against their parents and run away from home on a whim! They will never come to any good in the world, and sooner or later they will repent bitterly."

"Chat away, Cricket. I myself know that tomorrow at dawn I will leave, because if I stay I will have to do what all children do. I mean, they will send me to school and make me study whether I like it or not. But—I tell you this in confidence—studying is not for me at all. I would rather chase butterflies and climb trees to pluck birds from their nests."

"Poor little fool! You don't realize that in acting this way you will become a perfect donkey and everyone will mock you."

"Oh, shut up, you ill-talking Cricket!" shouted Pinocchio. And furious, he jumped up, grabbed a wooden hammer from the bench, and threw it at the Talking Cricket.

Maybe he hadn't intended to hit him. But unfortunately, he hit him on the head with such force that the poor Cricket made a last *cri-cri-cri* and then stayed stuck to the wall, dead stiff.

CHAPTER 5

Pinocchio is hungry and looks for an egg to make an omelet; but before he can prepare the omelet, the "egg" flies out the window.

It was nearly night. Pinocchio had an empty feeling in his stomach and remembered that he hadn't eaten anything.

This empty feeling in children grows rapidly. Soon Pinocchio was running around the room, looking in all of the cupboards, inspecting the shelves in search of a little dried bread, a crumb, a bone for the dog, leftover moldy polenta, a fish bone, or a cherry pit—whatever he could put in his mouth; but he found nothing, absolutely nothing, nothing, nothing.

Desperate, he began to cry. "The Talking Cricket was right. I shouldn't have rebelled against my papa or run away from home. Oh, what a wretched sickness to be hungry!"

But there in the dust he saw something white and round, like a chicken egg. He leaped toward it. It was indeed an egg. The puppet's joy was indescribable. As if in a dream, he turned the egg round and round in his hands, caressing and kissing it, saying, "And now, how am I going to cook it? An omelet? Soft boiled? Poached? Wouldn't that be just as tasty? Yes, and faster too. I want to eat so badly."

No sooner said than done. He put a pan over the hot coals and poured in a little water. When the water began to boil, he broke the shell. But instead of the yolk of an egg, out came a little Chick, quite happy and very polite. It curtsied and said, "Thank you a thousand times, Mr. Pinocchio, for saving me the trouble of breaking my shell myself. Make sure to say hello to your family."

Then the Chick spread its wings, flew out the open window up into the sky, and disappeared.

The poor puppet just stood there motionless with his eyes fixed, his mouth open, and the broken eggshell in his hand. When the shock passed, he began to cry, shout, and stamp his feet on the ground in despair. "The Talking Cricket was right!" he shouted. "If I hadn't run away from home and if my papa was still here, I wouldn't be dying of hunger! Oh, what a dreadful disease is hunger!"

And because his stomach rumbled more than ever and he didn't know how to satisfy it, he thought he would go out into the neighborhood to see if he could find a charitable person who would give him some bread.

CHAPTER 6

Pinocchio falls asleep with his feet on the stove, and the next morning his feet are completely burned off.

It was a wild and stormy night. The thunder was tremendous and the lightning so bright that the sky seemed ablaze. A bitter, blustery wind whistled angrily, causing the trees to creak and groan and raising an immense cloud of dust that swept over the land.

Pinocchio was afraid of thunder and lightning, but hunger was stronger than fear. He pushed open the door, took off running at top speed, and arrived in the village in a hundred bounds with his tongue hanging out and panting for breath like a dog chasing a cat.

But he found the village dark and deserted. The shops were closed, house windows and doors were shut, and there was not so much as a cat in the street. It seemed like a land of the dead.

Overwhelmed by desperation and hunger, Pinocchio took hold of a house bell and began to ring it with all his might. "This will bring somebody," he said to himself.

And so it did. A little old man with a nightcap on his head appeared at a window in an irritated mood.

"What do you want at this hour?"

"Would you be kind enough to give me a little bread?"

"Wait there. I'll be back directly," said the little old man, thinking he was dealing with one of those rascally boys who amuse themselves at night by ringing house bells to rouse respectable people who are sleeping quietly.

After a minute the window was opened again, and the little old man shouted, "Come underneath and hold out your cap."

Pinocchio took his cap off immediately; but as he held it out, an enormous basin of water poured down on him, soaking him from head to foot.

He returned home like a wet chicken, overcome with fatigue and hunger. Having no longer any strength to stand, he sat down and rested his damp muddy feet on a stove full of burning embers, and there he fell asleep.

While Pinocchio slept, his feet, which were wooden, caught fire; and little by little they burned away until there was nothing left but cinders.

Pinocchio snored away as if his feet belonged to someone else. At last at daybreak he was awakened by a knock on the door.

"Who is there?" he asked, yawning and rubbing his eyes.

"It is I!" answered a voice.

And the voice was that of Geppetto.

CHAPTER 7

*Geppetto returns home and gives Pinocchio
the breakfast that he had bought for himself.*

Poor Pinocchio, whose eyes were still half shut from sleep, had not yet discovered that his feet were burned off. The moment he heard his father's voice he slipped off his stool to run and open the door, but he fell flat on the floor.

"Open the door!" shouted Geppetto from the street.

"Dear Papa, I cannot," answered the puppet, crying and rolling about on the ground.

Geppetto climbed up the wall and got in through the window. When he saw Pinocchio lying on the ground without any feet, he was quite overcome.

"My little Pinocchio! How did you manage to burn off your feet?"

"I don't know, Papa, but believe me, it has been a terrible night that I will remember as long as I live. It lightninged and thundered, and I was very hungry." Pinocchio recounted his adventures and how when he returned, he had put his feet on the stove to dry them. "Then you came home and found my feet were burned off; and I am still hungry, but I no longer have any feet. Boohoohoohoo!" And poor Pinocchio began to cry and wail so loudly that he could be heard five miles away.

Geppetto had only understood one thing from this jumbled account: the puppet was dying of hunger. So he took three pears from his pocket and gave them to Pinocchio.

"I bought these three pears for my meal, but I will give them to you willingly."

"If you want me to eat them, be kind enough to peel them for me."

"Peel them?" said Geppetto, astonished. "I would never have thought, my boy, that you were so dainty and particular. That is a bad thing! In this world we should learn to like and eat everything. You never know what may happen."

"I will never eat fruit that has not been peeled," replied Pinocchio.

So the good Geppetto peeled the three pears and carefully put the peels on a corner of the table.

Having eaten the first pear in two bites, Pinocchio was about to throw away the core; but Geppetto caught hold of his arm and said, "Don't throw it away. In this world everything may be of use."

"For sure I will never eat the core," shouted the puppet.

"Who knows? Anything is possible," Geppetto said calmly.

And so the three cores, instead of being thrown out the window, were placed on the corner of the table with the three peels.

Having gobbled up the three pears, Pinocchio began to wail again. "I'm still hungry," he whined.

"But, my boy, I have nothing more to give you except the peels and cores of the three pears."

"That's too bad," said Pinocchio. "If there is nothing else, I will eat a peel."

And he began to chew it. At first he made a face, but then he ate the peels one right after another; and after that he even ate the cores. When he had eaten everything, he clapped his hands to his sides with satisfaction. "Ah! Now I feel better," he said joyfully.

"And you see," observed Geppetto, "that I was right when I told you not to be so particular. We can never know, my dear boy, what may happen to us. Anything is possible. . . ."

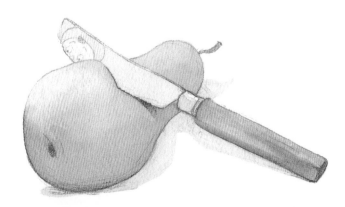

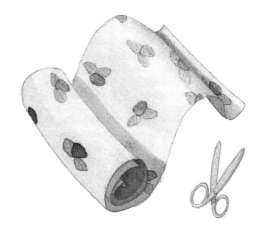

CHAPTER 8

Geppetto makes Pinocchio new feet and sells his own coat
to buy a spelling book for Pinocchio.

Geppetto's heart filled with sorrow at seeing his poor Pinocchio in such a pitiful state. He took his tools and two small pieces of well-seasoned wood and set to work diligently.

In less than an hour the feet were finished. Geppetto fastened the feet in place, and Pinocchio, crazy with delight, leaped and cavorted around.

"To reward you for what you have done for me, I will go to school at once."

"Good boy."

"But to go to school I will need some clothes."

Geppetto was poor and had not so much as a penny in his pocket. He made Pinocchio a little jacket out of flowered paper, a pair of shoes from the bark of a tree, and a cap from a crust of bread.

Pinocchio ran to look at himself in a crock of water, and he was so pleased with his appearance that he strutted about like a peacock. "I look like a real gentleman! But to go to school I am missing something essential. I have no spelling book."

"You are right. But what shall we do to get one?"

"It's easy. We go to the bookseller and buy it."

"And how will we pay for it? I have no money," said Geppetto. Suddenly he got up, put on his old coat, all patched and darned, and ran out of the house.

He returned shortly, holding in his hand a spelling book for Pinocchio, but his old coat was gone. The poor man was in his shirtsleeves, and it was snowing outdoors.

"And the coat, Papa?"

"I sold it."

"Why did you sell it?"

"Because I found it too warm."

Pinocchio understood in an instant; and having a good heart, he sprang up, threw his arms around Geppetto's neck, and kissed him again and again.

CHAPTER 9

Pinocchio sells his spelling book so that he can go to a puppet show.

When it stopped snowing, Pinocchio set off for school with his fine spelling book under his arm. "Today at school I will learn to read; tomorrow I'll learn to write; the day after tomorrow I will know how to count. Then with my knowledge I will earn a great deal of money, and the first thing I will buy with the money in my pocket will be a beautiful new cloth coat for my papa."

While telling himself all of this with great emotion, Pinocchio heard, from far away, the sound of fifes and a drumbeat. *Fi-fi-fi, fi-fi-fi. Boom-boom-boom-boom-boom.*

"What can that music be? It's too bad I have to go to school, otherwise . . ." And he stood there perplexed by his choice between school and the fifes.

"Let's say that today I go and hear the fifes, and tomorrow I go to school."

He ran off as fast as he could and found himself in the middle of a square full of people crowding round a wood-framed booth covered with a curtain of a thousand colors.

"What is that booth?" Pinocchio asked a little boy from the village.

"Read the sign—it's all written there—and then you'll know."

"I would read it willingly, except that as it happens, I don't know how to read."

"Bravo, blockhead! Then I will read it to you. On this poster in fiery red letters is written: 'GRAND THEATER OF PUPPETS.'"

"How much does it cost to go in?"

"Four centesimi."

"Could you loan me four centesimi until tomorrow?"

"I would lend them to you willingly, but as it happens I can't today." The little boy sneered.

"I'll sell you my jacket for four centesimi," replied Pinocchio.

"What am I supposed to do with a jacket made of colored paper?"

"Then take my shoes."

"They're only good for lighting a fire."

"And my cap. How much would you give me for it?"

"That would be truly wonderful to have," the boy mocked. "A cap made of bread."

Pinocchio had one last offer to make, but he hesitated. At last he said, "Could you give me four centesimi for this brand-new spelling book?"

"I'll take it for four centesimi," said a ragman who had overheard their conversation.

The book was sold on the spot.

CHAPTER 10

The marionettes recognize Pinocchio as one of their own and receive him with delight, but just when the merriment reaches its high point, Mangiafoco the puppeteer shows up and Pinocchio will likely come to a bad end.

When Pinocchio entered the theater, the curtain had already risen and the show had begun.

Onstage, Harlequin and Punchinello were, as usual, quarreling and threatening to come to blows at any moment.

Suddenly Harlequin stopped. "Good heavens! Am I dreaming? Isn't that Pinocchio that I see over there?" he said with gusto.

"It's really Pinocchio," Punchinello said at his turn.

"Pinocchio, come here," shouted Harlequin, "and throw yourself into the arms of your wooden brothers!"

At this warm welcome, Pinocchio jumped from his seat. In a single leap he was in the first row. Another leap propelled him onto the head of the orchestra conductor and, from there, directly onto the stage.

It's difficult to imagine the overwhelming demonstrations of affection that Pinocchio received from the actors and actresses of this puppet troupe.

The spectacle was truly moving. However, seeing that the play had come to a halt, the public grew impatient and shouted, "On with the play!"

At that moment appeared the master puppeteer, a huge man who was so ugly that the mere sight of him would kill a person. At his appearance the racket stopped abruptly. The audience held their breath. It was so still you could have heard a fly beating its wings. All of the puppets, male and female, trembled.

"Why did you come here to create pandemonium in my theater?" asked the puppeteer in the booming voice of an ogre with a bad head cold.

"It's not my fault, sir. I beg you to believe me."

"Enough! Tonight I'll settle with you." He was not speaking in vain because after the show the puppeteer went to his kitchen, where a whole sheep was being roasted for dinner. However, as he didn't have enough wood, he called Harlequin and Punchinello and said, "Bring me that puppet hanging on that nail."

At first Harlequin and Punchinello hesitated. But an evil look from their boss terrorized them so much that they obeyed. In a moment they returned carrying poor Pinocchio.

"Papa, Papa, save me! I don't want to die. I don't want to die," Pinocchio cried in despair.

CHAPTER 11

Mangiafoco sneezes and pardons Pinocchio, who then saves his friend Harlequin's life.

It's true that Mangiafoco looked terrifying, but deep down he was not a bad man. When Pinocchio was brought before him, he felt sorry for the puppet and began to sneeze violently. Harlequin smiled and leaned toward Pinocchio to whisper, "Good news, brother. The master has sneezed, a sign that he has compassion for you and you are saved."

When he finished sneezing, the puppeteer grumbled to Pinocchio, "Enough of this crying. Tell me if your mama and papa are still alive."

"Papa, yes. I never knew my mama."

"Evidently. Evidently. What a sorrow it would be for your poor old father if I were to have you thrown onto the burning coals. Poor man! I feel for him! . . . *Ah-choo, ah-choo, ah-choo*!" he sneezed three times.

"Bless you!" said Pinocchio.

"Thank you! All the same, compassion is due to me too, since as you see, I don't have any more wood to finish roasting my mutton. To tell you the truth, throwing you onto the fire would have been of great use to me! I will replace you with one of the puppets in my company. Ho there, Carabinieri! Bring me Harlequin."

Upset by this, Pinocchio threw himself at the puppeteer's feet and cried tears all over his beard. "Have pity, Mr. Mangiafoco. Pardon poor Harlequin."

"For him there can be no pardon. Since I spared you, he must be put on the fire, for I am determined that my mutton shall be well roasted."

"In that case," shouted Pinocchio proudly as he rose and threw away his bread crust cap, "in that case, I know my duty. Come on! Tie me up and throw me on the flames. It is not right that poor Harlequin, my true friend, should die for me!"

Mangiafoco was at first unmoved, but little by little he began to soften, and then he sneezed. After sneezing four or five times, he opened his arms affectionately. "You are a good, brave boy! Come give me a kiss."

Pinocchio ran into the puppeteer's arms. Climbing like a squirrel up the man's beard, he kissed him heartily on the end of his nose.

"Then the pardon is granted?" asked poor Harlequin in a faint voice that was scarcely audible.

"The pardon is granted!" answered Mangiafoco, sighing and shaking his head. "It's too bad, but tonight I have to be satisfied with half-cooked mutton. But next time, woe to he who comes along!"

CHAPTER 12

*Mangiafoco gives Pinocchio a present of five gold pieces for his father,
Geppetto; but instead of going to his father, Pinocchio allows himself to
be taken in by the Fox and the Cat and ends up going off with them.*

The next day, Mangiafoco took Pinocchio aside and asked him, "What does your father do, Pinocchio?"

"A poor man's trade. He had to sell his coat to buy me a spelling book."

"Poor devil! I feel sorry for him. Here are five gold coins. Go at once and take these coins to him."

Pinocchio thanked Mangiafoco again and again, then joyfully set off to return home. But he hadn't traveled five hundred meters when he met a blind Cat and a Fox who had one lame foot, who were going along helping each other like good companions in misfortune.

"Hello, Pinocchio," the Fox greeted him politely.

"How do you know my name?" said the astonished puppet.

"I know your father well. I saw him yesterday on his front steps. He was shaking with cold."

"Poor Papa. I am going to buy him a new coat." He showed the two companions what the puppeteer had given him.

"Would you like to double your money?" asked the Fox. "Instead of returning home, you must come with us to the Land of the Owls."

"No, I can't go. I want to find my papa, who awaits me."

"Too bad for you!" The Fox sighed. "By tomorrow your five coins could have become two thousand."

"As much as that? How is that possible?" Pinocchio's mouth dropped open in astonishment.

"I'll explain," said the Fox. "In the Land of the Owls, there is a field known as the Field of Miracles. In this field, you dig a shallow hole and put in, let's say, one gold coin. The next morning, return to the field and what will you find there? A magnificent tree covered with as many gold coins as there are kernels on an ear of corn in the middle of June."

"That's fantastic!" shouted Pinocchio, dancing around with joy. "Incredible." And forgetting his father and all of his good resolutions, he declared, "Okay, I'm going with you."

CHAPTER 13

*Pinocchio falls asleep at the Red Crawfish Inn and gets
some advice from the Talking Cricket.*

At nightfall, they arrived dead tired at the Red Crawfish Inn.

"Let's stop here awhile to eat something and to rest for an hour or two," said the Fox. "We'll start again at midnight to go to the Field of Miracles."

They all three sat down at a table, but no one had much appetite. The poor Cat could eat only thirty-five mullet fish with tomato sauce and four portions of Parmesan tripe. The Fox would have also willingly picked a little at his food; but the doctor had ordered him to follow a strict diet, so he had to content himself with a simple hare garnished with fat chickens. After the hare, he ordered a fricassee of partridges, rabbits, frogs, and lizards.

The one who ate the least was Pinocchio. The poor boy, whose thoughts were continually fixed on the Field of Miracles, suffered from anticipation-of-gold-coins indigestion. No sooner had Pinocchio gotten into bed than he fell asleep. He dreamed that he was in the middle of a field full of shrubs covered with clusters of gold coins. Just as he was stretching out his hand to pick a handful of those beautiful gold coins, someone knocked on the door. It was the innkeeper, who had come to tell him that midnight had struck.

"And my friends?" asked the puppet. "Are they ready?"

"Ready! Why, they left two hours ago."

"Did they pay for supper?"

"What are you thinking of? They are much too well educated to dream of offering such an insult to a gentleman like you."

"Too bad! It's an insult that would not have displeased me," said Pinocchio.

Pinocchio paid a gold coin for his supper and that of his companions, and then left. Outside the inn it was so pitch-dark that it was impossible to see a hand's length in front of him.

As he walked along, he saw a little insect shining dimly on the trunk of a tree, like the little flame in an oil lamp.

"Who are you?" asked Pinocchio.

"I am the ghost of the Talking Cricket," answered the insect in a low voice so weak and faint that it seemed to come from the Beyond.

"What do you want with me?" said the puppet.

"I want to give you some advice. Go back and take your father the four gold coins that you have left. He is weeping and in despair because you haven't returned to him."

"By tomorrow my papa will be a gentleman, because these four gold coins will become two thousand."

"My boy, never trust those who promise to make you rich in a day. They are either mad or rogues. Believe me, and go back."

"No, I am determined to go on."

"Remember that boys who are intent on following their own foolishness always end up repenting."

"Always the same stories! Good night, Cricket."

"Good night, Pinocchio. May heaven protect you from the dew and from bandits."

No sooner had he said these words than the Talking Cricket vanished like a light that has been blown out, and the road became darker than ever.

CHAPTER 14

Heedless of the Talking Cricket's advice, Pinocchio
finds himself face-to-face with bandits.

Grumbling to himself, Pinocchio resumed his journey. "That tiresome Cricket predicts that many misfortunes will befall me if I don't do as he says. I even risk meeting up with bandits, he says. Happily, I don't believe in bandits. As far as I'm concerned, they were invented by papas to scare their children."

Suddenly Pinocchio heard a slight rustle of leaves behind him. He quickly turned around. In the darkness, he saw two evil-looking figures completely enveloped in coal sacks.

"Bandits," he said to himself, and not knowing where to hide his gold pieces, he popped them into his mouth.

"Your money or your life!" the two bandits shouted together.

"Hand over your money or you are dead."

"And after we kill you, we will kill your father."

"No, no, not my poor papa!" cried Pinocchio in despair. As he spoke, the coins clinked in his mouth.

"Ah, you rascal! Your money—you've hidden it under your tongue. Spit it out now."

But Pinocchio remained stone still.

"Ah, pretending to be deaf, are you? Then leave it to us. We'll find a way to make you spit it out."

Then one of the bandits grabbed Pinocchio by the nose, and the other took him by the chin. They began to pull brutally, one up and the other down, trying to force him to open his mouth. But they didn't succeed. The puppet's mouth remained sealed shut.

Then the shorter bandit took out an ugly knife and tried to force it between Pinocchio's lips. But Pinocchio, quick as lightning, bit off the bandit's hand. When he spit it out, he was astonished to see that it was a cat's paw.

Bolstered by his success, he managed to free himself from his attackers and escape across the fields. The bandits ran

after him like two hunting dogs chasing a hare. Even the one who had lost a paw ran on one leg, and no one ever knew how he managed to do it.

CHAPTER 15

The bandits continue chasing Pinocchio. After catching him,
they hang him from the branch of an oak tree.

Discouraged, the puppet was on the verge of giving up when he saw in the distance, standing out amid the dark green of the trees, a small house as white as snow.

"If only I have enough breath to reach that house," he thought, "perhaps I will be saved."

Two hours later, he arrived breathless at the door of the house and knocked.

A pretty girl with blue hair and a face as pale as a statue appeared at the window. In a voice that seemed to come from Beyond, she murmured, "In this house there is no one. They are all dead. I too am dead."

With these words the girl disappeared and the window closed without a sound.

"Oh beautiful girl with blue hair, open the door for pity's sake. Help a poor boy who is being chased by ban—"

But he couldn't finish the word. Someone had seized his collar, and the same two horrible voices said menacingly, "You will not get away from us again!"

Without delay they tied his arms behind him, passed a noose around his throat, and hung him from the branch of a tree called the Great Oak.

"We are leaving you," they told him. "But we will return tomorrow. By then we hope you will have the courtesy to die completely and open your mouth wide."

Then they left.

No sooner had they gone than the tempestuous north wind rose up and began to batter the poor puppet as he hung, swinging him violently like the clapper of a wedding bell. The violent swinging gave Pinocchio great pain, and the noose grew tighter round his throat and took away his breath.

Little by little, Pinocchio's vision clouded. Feeling death upon him, he still imagined that some kind person would save him. But after waiting and hoping, he understood that no one, no one, would help him. Then he remembered his poor father. Thinking that he was about to die, he stammered, "Oh, Papa, Papa! If only you were here!"

Then his breath gave out and he could say no more. He shut his eyes, opened his mouth, let his legs drop, gave a last long shudder, and hung stiff and senseless at the end of his rope.

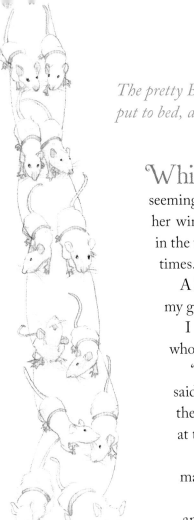

CHAPTER 16

While poor Pinocchio hung from the branch of the Great Oak, seeming more dead than alive, the pretty Blue-Haired Girl returned to her window. Seeing the unfortunate puppet hanging by the neck dancing in the wind at the end of his rope, she felt pity. She clapped her hands three times.

A large Falcon came to perch on the windowsill. "What are the orders of my gracious Fairy?" asked the Falcon, respectfully bowing his head.

I should tell you that the Blue-Haired Girl was, in fact, a good Fairy who had been living in this wood for more than a thousand years.

"Do you see the puppet hanging from the branch of the Great Oak?" said the Fairy. "Fly there immediately and use your strong beak to untie the knot that holds him in the air. Then lay him down gently on the grass at the foot of the oak."

The Fairy clapped her hands twice. This time there appeared a magnificent Poodle that walked upright on his hind legs like a human.

"Quick," said the Fairy, "take the most beautiful carriage in my stable and drive to the woods. At the Great Oak, you will find a puppet lying on the grass, half dead. Take him up with care, gently lay him on the cushions, and bring him to me. Do you understand?"

The Poodle sped off, and shortly afterward a beautiful sky blue carriage drawn by two hundred little white mice came out of the stable. Seated on the coach box, the Poodle cracked his whip.

Within a quarter hour the carriage returned. The Fairy took the poor puppet by the collar, carried him to a bedroom, then called the most famous doctors in the area.

One after another they arrived: a Crow, an Owl, and a Talking Cricket. Assembling them around the bed where Pinocchio lay, the Fairy said, "I would like for you to tell me, signors, if this unfortunate puppet is dead or alive."

The Crow advanced first. "In my opinion, the puppet is already quite dead; but if he should not be dead, then it would be a sign that he is still alive."

"I regret," responded the Owl, "that I must contradict my illustrious friend and colleague the Crow; but, in my opinion, on the contrary, the puppet is alive. Evidently, if by some mishap he was not alive, then that would be the indisputable sign that he is dead."

"And you?" the Fairy asked the Talking Cricket. "You say nothing?"

"As for myself," said the Cricket, "I believe that for a doctor who doesn't know what he's talking about, the best thing to do is remain silent. Moreover, this puppet is not unknown to me. I have known him for a long time! This puppet is a no-good rascal, a naughty scamp, a lazy good-for-nothing, and a vagabond. On top of that, he is a disobedient child who will cause his father to die of chagrin."

At that moment there arose the sound of sobbing. Imagine everyone's surprise when the sheet was raised and all could see that it was Pinocchio who was weeping.

"When a dead person cries, it signifies that he will get well," declared the Crow with solemnity.

"I deplore that I must again contradict my illustrious friend and colleague," the Owl interrupted, "but, in my opinion, when a dead person cries, it means he is unhappy to be dead."

CHAPTER 17

Pinocchio will eat the sugar but will not take his medicine. However, when he sees the grave diggers arrive to carry him away, he takes his medicine. Then he tells a lie and his nose grows longer.

When the three doctors had left, the Fairy took care of Pinocchio. Bending over him, she touched his forehead and realized that he had a high fever. She dissolved some white powder in half a glass of water and held it out to the puppet. "Drink this and you will be healed in a short time," she told him tenderly.

Pinocchio looked at the glass and, pouting, asked in a whining voice, "Is it sweet or bitter?"

"Bitter, but it will do you good," said the Fairy. "When you have drunk it, I will give you a sugar cube to take away the taste."

Pinocchio reluctantly took the glass, held his nose over it, and finally announced, "It's too bitter! Too bitter! I can't drink it."

"You will regret it, my boy. The fever can cause you to die. Aren't you afraid of dying?"

"Not at all. It's better to die than to drink that dreadful mixture."

At that moment the door opened wide, and four Rabbits entered carrying a little coffin on their shoulders.

"What do you want of me?" screamed Pinocchio, sitting up in a fright.

"We came to get you," said the largest Rabbit.

"Get me? But I'm not dead yet! Oh Fairy, my good Fairy," begged the puppet, "bring me the glass right now! Please hurry, for pity's sake. I don't want to die. I don't want to die. . . ." Pinocchio took the glass in both hands and emptied its contents in one gulp. Several minutes later, he jumped up from his bed, cured for good. The Rabbits left, grumbling.

"Good," said the Fairy. "Now tell me how you found yourself a prisoner of the bandits."

Pinocchio told her about his adventures, how the bandits had tried to steal his coins from him and how he had hidden his coins under his tongue.

"These coins," asked the Fairy, "where are they now?"

"I lost them!"

This was a lie, and Pinocchio's nose, already a nose of some consequence, grew instantly longer.

"And where did you lose them?"

"In the woods."

This was a second lie. Pinocchio's nose grew even longer.

"If you lost them in the woods, let's go look for them and we'll find them."

"Oh, yes! Now I recall," replied the puppet, sounding confused. "The four gold coins, I didn't lose them. I didn't pay attention, and I swallowed them with your medicine."

At this third lie, Pinocchio's nose grew so much that he could no longer turn his head.

The Fairy looked at him and laughed.

Ashamed, not knowing where to hide himself, Pinocchio tried to leave the room; but his nose had become so long that he couldn't get out the door.

CHAPTER 18

*Pinocchio meets the Fox and the Cat again and goes off with
them to plant his four gold coins in the Field of Miracles.*

To teach him a lesson, the Fairy let Pinocchio cry and wail. But when she saw him overcome by despair, she felt sorry for him. She clapped her hands, and a huge flock of woodpeckers flew in the window. They immediately perched on Pinocchio's nose and began to peck at it with such zeal that in a few minutes his gigantic, ridiculous nose was restored to its usual size.

"What a good Fairy you are," said the puppet, drying his eyes, "and I love you so much."

"I love you too," said the Fairy, "and if you wish, you may stay with me."

"I would do so willingly, but what will become of my papa?"

"I think of everything. Your papa has been notified. He will be here before night comes."

"Really?" shouted Pinocchio, jumping for joy. "Then, if you permit, I would like to go meet him. I can't wait to embrace him!"

"Go then, but pay attention not to get lost."

Pinocchio left, and as soon as he was in the forest, he began to run like a deer. But guess who appeared on the road? The Fox and the Cat, his two traveling companions.

"Why, it's our dear Pinocchio!" exclaimed the Fox. "What are you doing here?"

"It's a long story that I will tell you when I have time," the puppet told them. "Now I'm waiting for my papa, who ought to arrive at any moment."

"And the coins?"

"I still have them. They are in my pocket, except for the one that I used to pay the innkeeper."

"When one thinks that instead of four coins, you could have a thousand or even two thousand as soon as tomorrow. Why don't you come with us to plant them in the Field of Miracles?"

Pinocchio hesitated because he thought about the good Fairy and Geppetto and the warnings of the Talking Cricket. But he did what all children do who don't have a speck of good judgment; that is, he finally said to the Fox and the Cat with a little shake of his head, "All right, I'll go with you."

All three of them left together.

After a good half hour of walking, they stopped in a field that looked just like any other field.

"Here we are," the Fox said to the puppet. "Bend down and dig a little hole in the ground for your gold coins."

Pinocchio obeyed. He dug the hole, dropped in the four remaining coins, and covered them up with a little bit of dirt.

"Now," the Fox went on, "go to the pond nearby, fill a bucket with water, and water the spot where you planted the seeds."

Pinocchio went to the pond. As he had no bucket, he took off one of his shoes and filled it with water. After watering his seeds, he asked, "Is there something else to do?"

"Nothing more," the Fox assured him. "Everyone can leave. But if you return in twenty minutes, you will find that a young tree has sprung up, and its branches will be weighed down with gold coins."

They bid good-bye to Pinocchio, wished him a good harvest, and went on their way.

Pinocchio counted the minutes one by one. When it seemed to him that it was time, he hurried back to the Field of Miracles and went to the hole where he had planted his coins. Nothing! There was nothing!

And then he heard a big laugh. Raising his head, he saw a Parrot preening the few plumes that he had left.

"Why are you laughing?" Pinocchio asked.

"I laugh at all fools who are ready to do whatever idiocy anyone tells them to do and let themselves be taken advantage of by those more cunning than they are."

"Are you talking about me?"

"Yes, I'm talking about you, my poor Pinocchio, who is foolish enough to believe that you can plant and harvest money the way you plant beans or pumpkins. You should know that in your absence the Cat and the Fox returned, dug up the coins, and left with them."

Speechless, not wanting to believe what the Parrot told him, Pinocchio dropped to the ground and began digging with his fingernails at the spot he had just watered. He dug and dug and dug until he had made a hole deep enough for a haystack. But the coins? There were none. They were no longer there.

In despair Pinocchio ran to the neighboring town and went straight to the courthouse to denounce the two scoundrels who had just robbed him.

The judge was a Gorilla, an old Ape whose age made him seem respectable. He listened to Pinocchio with kindness. Then when Pinocchio had nothing left to say, he reached out his arm and rang a bell. Immediately two Mastiffs in police uniforms entered the room.

The judge, showing Pinocchio to the police, told them, "Someone stole four gold coins from this poor devil. Seize him then and take him immediately to prison."

This unexpected sentence terrified the puppet, who wanted to protest. But the police officers, in order to avoid any useless waste of time, prevented him from speaking and threw him into prison.

There Pinocchio stayed for four long months.

CHAPTER 20

Freed from prison, Pinocchio sets off to return to the Fairy's house, but first a horrible Snake bars his way and then he is caught in a trap.

Pinocchio's joy at being freed was indescribable. Without delay he left town and returned to the road that led to the Fairy's.

"What a mess I've gotten myself into," he said to himself as he ran along. "But I didn't steal. Is Papa still waiting for me? Will I find him at the Fairy's house? And will the Fairy forgive me for my bad behavior?"

Suddenly Pinocchio stopped and took four steps backward. A large Snake stretched its whole length across the road. His skin was yellow, his eyes were as red as fire, and his pointed tail smoked like a chimney. Retreating as far as possible, Pinocchio sat on a stone and waited for the old Snake to move along and make room to pass. He waited one hour, two hours, three hours. . . . The snake was still there.

Mustering his courage, Pinocchio approached. "Excuse me, Mr. Snake," he said in a tiny, pleading voice, "but would you be good enough to move a little to one side, just enough so that I might pass by?"

The Snake, who up to that moment had been sprightly and full of life, became motionless and almost rigid. He shut his eyes, and his tail stopped smoking.

"Could he really be dead?" Pinocchio wondered, and clapped his hands in happiness. But he had no sooner raised his foot to step over the dead Snake than the Snake suddenly rose up. Flustered, Pinocchio leaped backward and in his terror tripped and fell to the ground. He fell so awkwardly that he wound up with his head stuck in the mud and his legs kicking in the air.

Seeing the puppet upside down wiggling in a frenzy, the Snake was overcome with uncontrollable laughter and broke a blood vessel in his chest. And this time he really did die.

Pinocchio set off running again, but on the way he got so awfully hungry he couldn't stand it. He went into a vineyard to gather a bunch of grapes. Suddenly, *CRACK!* Pinocchio felt two sharp steel blades bite his leg. The poor puppet had stumbled into a trap.

CHAPTER 21

*Pinocchio is freed from the trap by a farmer who then
compels him to act as "watchdog" of his chicken coop.*

𝒫inocchio began to cry and scream, but his tears and cries were useless since there was no house in sight and no one passed by on the road.

Night fell.

Pinocchio was on the verge of fainting from the pain of the trap cutting his legs and also from his fear at finding himself in such a situation, alone in the dark in the middle of a field. But just at that moment, a Firefly flittered above his head. "Oh, beautiful Firefly," said Pinocchio, "would you be so kind as to relieve me from the pain of this trap?"

"Poor child!" said the Firefly, gazing at Pinocchio with pity. "What did you do to get caught between these blades?"

"I went into the field to gather two clusters of grapes and . . ."

"Are these your grapes?"

"No . . ."

"And so? Who taught you to take what belongs to another?"

"I was hungry."

"That is not a sufficient reason, my boy, to try to take what doesn't belong to you."

"It's true! It's true!" admitted Pinocchio, who was still crying. "I won't do it again."

Their conversation was interrupted by the muffled sound of approaching footsteps.

It was the owner of the property. Walking stealthily, he was coming to see if his trap had caught one of the Martens that came each night to eat his chickens.

How astonished he was when he discovered that instead of a Marten, he had trapped a boy.

"Ah, dirty little thief!" shouted the angry farmer. "So you're the one who's been stealing my chickens."

"No, no, it's not me!" sobbed Pinocchio. "I only came into the field to take a few grapes."

"Whoever steals grapes can very well also steal chickens. I am going to give you a good lesson that you will remember for a long time."

And opening the trap, the farmer lifted the puppet by the neck and carried him to his house as if he was a baby lamb.

When he got to the courtyard of his house, the farmer dropped Pinocchio on the ground and pinned him down with his foot. "Now it's late and I'm going to bed. We'll settle this tomorrow. In the meantime, since my dog died today, you will take his place and be my watchdog."

Then he fastened a thick, nail-studded collar around Pinocchio's neck and adjusted it so that the puppet couldn't slip his head out. A long chain was hooked to the collar, the other end of which was attached to the wall.

"If it rains tonight, you can go sleep in the kennel. You'll find straw there—it was my dog's bed for four years. And if thieves show up, don't forget to bark."

After dispensing this last word of advice, the farmer went into the house and closed and bolted the door behind him. Poor Pinocchio remained lying there on the ground in the courtyard more dead than alive because of the cold, his hunger, and his fear.

Pinocchio had been sleeping soundly in the kennel for more than two hours when he was awakened around midnight by whispers and murmurs. He peeked outside. There was a group of four dark-furred animals. They looked a bit like cats, but these cats were, in reality, Martens, animals who are particularly fond of eggs and young chickens.

Leaving his companions, one of the Martens approached the kennel.

"Good evening, Melampo," he said under his breath.

"I'm not Melampo," said the puppet. "My name is Pinocchio."

"Where's Melampo? Where is the old dog who lives in this kennel?"

"He died this morning."

"Dead? Poor beast! He was so good! But now that I have a look at you, you appear to be a very friendly dog too."

"Sorry, but I'm not a dog! I'm a puppet."

"But you are acting like a watchdog."

"Unfortunately, yes. It's my punishment."

"Good. In that case, I propose that we renew the agreement I had with Melampo. We come once a week, as before, to visit the henhouse, from which we will take eight chickens. Seven are for us, and we will give you the eighth. But—listen well—*only* on the condition that you pretend to sleep and don't get any ideas about barking or waking up the farmer. We understand each other, don't we?"

"Only too well!"

The four Martens, assured after this, took off toward the chicken coop. But no sooner had they entered than they heard the door close with a loud noise.

Pinocchio had just closed the door on them. Then he began to bark, exactly as a real watchdog would have done.

The barking woke the farmer, who jumped out of bed, grabbed his rifle, and leaned out the window. "What is going on?" he cried.

"The chicken thieves are here," answered Pinocchio.

"I'll be there right away."

The farmer ran to the henhouse, caught the Martens, and put them in a gunnysack.

"Bravo, my boy!" exclaimed the farmer, giving Pinocchio a friendly tap on the shoulder. "To show you my gratitude, I will give you your freedom. You can return to your home."

And he removed the dog collar.

CHAPTER 23

Pinocchio mourns the death of the pretty Blue-Haired Girl. Then he meets a Pigeon who takes him to the seashore. There he plunges into the sea to save his papa, Geppetto.

As soon as Pinocchio was rid of the collar choking him, he set off again on the road to the Fairy's. But he could not find her house. In the clearing where she had lived there was only a simple marble stone on which were written these sad words:

> HERE LIES THE BLUE-HAIRED GIRL,
> WHO DIED FROM CHAGRIN
> AFTER HAVING BEEN ABANDONED
> BY HER LITTLE BROTHER PINOCCHIO.

I leave to you to imagine Pinocchio's reaction when he had more or less deciphered this inscription. He threw himself on the ground and covered the stone with kisses, sobbing all the while. He cried all night. At sunrise he was still crying. He cried so much that at dawn he had no more tears left in his eyes. His heartbreaking lament echoed all across the neighboring hills.

At this moment a large Pigeon, who had stopped for a moment to stretch his wings, called out, "Tell me, young man, what are you doing lying on the ground?"

"Can't you see?" answered Pinocchio. "I'm crying."

"Tell me," the Pigeon asked, "do you know, by chance, among your friends, a puppet named Pinocchio?"

Pinocchio jumped to his feet. "Pinocchio? Did you say Pinocchio? Pinocchio, that's me!"

The Pigeon, who was bigger than a turkey, flew down swiftly to land near him. "Then you would know Geppetto?"

"Know him? But he's my papa! Did he talk to you about me? Is he still alive?"

"Three days ago he was at the seashore. He had made himself a rowboat to travel the world in search of you. If you wish, I will take you to him."

Without a moment's hesitation, Pinocchio jumped onto the big Pigeon's back. He wrapped his arms tightly around the neck of his feathered mount, and they flew all day. The next morning they landed on the beach. The Pigeon let Pinocchio down and flew off at once.

The beach was filled with people shouting and gesturing as they looked out to sea.

"What's going on?" Pinocchio asked an old woman.

"A poor man has set off in a boat in search of his son on the other side of the ocean. But the sea is bad today, and his rowboat is in danger of sinking."

Pinocchio stared out to sea. "It's my papa!" he shouted. "It's my papa! I'm going to save my papa!"

Because he was made of wood, Pinocchio floated easily. Moreover, he swam like a fish. For a long time those onshore could see a leg or an arm appear and then disappear in the waves farther and farther from the shore until at last they saw nothing.

"Poor boy!" The fishermen sighed. And they went home murmuring a prayer.

CHAPTER 24

*Pinocchio arrives at an island called the Island of the Busy Bees
and finds the Fairy again.*

In the hope of saving his poor papa, Pinocchio swam all night. At dawn he glimpsed a long strip of land emerging from the sea. He mustered all of his strength to reach it, but in vain. However, happily for him, a giant wave catapulted him onto the sandy bank.

"Oof! Once again I had a narrow escape."

After he had dried his clothes, he set off at a brisk pace along a path, and in a half hour he arrived in a little village called the Village of Busy Bees. The streets were filled with people who ran in every direction, each of them with something to do. Search as one might, one couldn't see an idle person anywhere.

"I understand," lazy Pinocchio concluded immediately. "This country is not for me! I was not born to work!"

But he hadn't eaten anything in a long time, and hunger tormented him. He was wondering what to do when a nice young woman appeared, carrying two pitchers full of water.

"Good lady, would you permit me to drink a swallow of water from one of your pitchers?" asked Pinocchio, whose throat burned from thirst.

"Drink, my boy," said the young woman, setting her load on the ground.

Pinocchio drank like a sponge. Then, wiping his mouth, he murmured, "Now I'm no longer thirsty. But what shall I do about my hunger?"

Hearing his words, the kind woman said, "If you will help me by carrying one of these pitchers, I will give you a nice piece of bread when we arrive at my house."

Pinocchio stared at the big pitcher without responding.

"And with the bread I will serve you a plate of cauliflower in oil and vinegar," said the young woman.

Pinocchio looked again at the pitcher without deciding.

"And after the cauliflower, you will have earned an almond candy."

The prospect of such a treat was more than Pinocchio could resist. "All right," he said. "I will carry one of the pitchers to your house."

The pitcher was heavy and Pinocchio didn't have enough strength to carry it in his arms, so he had to carry it on his head.

Once they arrived, the nice young woman had Pinocchio sit at a small table already set and placed before him the bread, cauliflower, and almond candy.

Pinocchio did not just eat; he devoured. As his hunger eased, he raised his head to thank his benefactress; but he had barely looked at her when he gasped a long "Oooh" of surprise. He sat there frozen, his eyes wide, his fork in the air, and his mouth full of cauliflower.

"To what do I owe such astonishment?" The young woman laughed.

"You are . . . ," babbled Pinocchio. "You are . . . you are . . . you resemble . . . I remember clearly . . . yes, yes, the same eyes, the same hair . . . yes, yes, blue hair like hers. Oh, my dear Fairy! My very own Fairy! Tell me that it's you, that it's really you!"

And shedding hot tears, Pinocchio threw himself to the ground and wrapped his arms around the knees of the mysterious young woman..

CHAPTER 25

Tired of being a puppet and wanting to become a good boy,
Pinocchio promises the Fairy that he will improve and study.

The kind young woman had begun by pretending that she was not the Fairy with blue hair, but when she realized that she was discovered, she admitted it.

"Clever puppet! How did you recognize me?"

"It's simply because I love you so much," Pinocchio told her. "From now on I want so much to call you Mama. For such a long time I've been wanting to have a mama like other children. Besides, I'm tired of being a puppet. It's time for me to become a real child."

"And so you will," said the Fairy. "But you must deserve it."

"What do I have to do?"

"It's very simple. All you have to do is agree to be a good little boy."

"Which, perhaps, I am not . . ."

"Indeed! A good boy is obedient. You, on the contrary . . ."

"And me, I never obey."

"A good boy loves to study and work. You, on the contrary . . ."

"And me, on the contrary, I loaf around and am good for nothing much of the time."

"A good boy always tells the truth. . . ."

"And me, always lies."

"A good boy doesn't complain about going to school. . . ."

"As for me, school makes me sick. But now I want to change."

"Do you promise me?"

"I promise. I want to become a well-behaved child and to make my papa proud. In fact, where is he, my poor papa, right now?"

"I don't know."

"Will I have the happiness of seeing him again and giving him big kisses?"

"I believe so. I am even certain of it."

The Fairy's answer made Pinocchio feel beside himself with happiness. He took her hands and kissed them. Then looking at her, his eyes filled with love, he asked, "And so, my little mama, you are not dead?"

"Apparently not," answered the Fairy, smiling.

"If you knew how my throat tightened and what grief I felt when I read 'Here lies.'"

"I know. That's why I forgave you. I understood that you have a good heart; and when a child has a good heart, one can always hope that he will find his way again, even if he is a rascal and has taken up bad habits. That is why I came here looking for you. I will be your mama."

"How wonderful!" shouted Pinocchio, jumping for joy.

"But you will obey me and do everything I tell you."

"I will study, I will work, I will do everything you want, because the life of a puppet is not for me anymore. I want, no matter what it costs, to become a child like other children. You promised me I could, didn't you?"

"I promised. From now on, it's up to you."

CHAPTER 26

Pinocchio goes to the seashore with his school friends to see the terrible Shark.

The next day Pinocchio set off for school.

Imagine the reaction of all the naughty pupils when they saw a puppet enter their classroom. Everyone burst out laughing. Some snatched his cap. Others tugged his jacket from behind or drew an ink mustache under his nose. Some even tied strings to his legs and arms to make him dance.

At first Pinocchio acted as if he wasn't bothered and stayed calm. But his patience had its limits. Finally he shouted, "Enough! I didn't come here to be made fun of. I respect others, and others should respect me."

"Bravo! You talk like a book!" shouted one of the mean boys, and he laughed even louder.

One of them, even bolder than the others, tried to grab the puppet's nose. But he didn't succeed because Pinocchio kicked him hard on the shin.

"Ai! Ai! He has terrifically hard feet!" the boy complained, rubbing his leg.

"And his elbows are even harder than his feet," said another.

Kicking with his foot and jabbing with his elbows had a strange effect: Pinocchio won the respect and sympathy of all of the pupils, who then set about befriending him.

The teacher praised him because he was so attentive and studious. He was always the first to arrive at school and the last to get up from his bench when the lesson was over.

Pinocchio's only problem was that he had some friends who were troublemakers. They were well-known for not liking to work, and they didn't do well at school.

It happened that one day on his way to school, Pinocchio met some of these friends.

"Have you heard the news?" they asked. "In the sea not far from here, there is a Shark as big as a mountain. We're going to the beach to see it. Do you want to come with us?"

"No, not me. I'm going to school."

"School? Not important! We'll go tomorrow. One lesson more or less won't change anything; we will always be donkeys."

"And the teacher? What will he say?" said Pinocchio.

"The teacher can say what he wants. Anyway, he's paid to complain all day."

"And my mama?"

"Mamas never know what's going on," the little pests assured him.

"Okay, here's what I'll do," Pinocchio decided. "I want to see this Shark too. But I'll go after school."

"Blockhead!" said one of the boys. "Do you really believe that a fish of such a size is going to stay where he is just for your pleasure? As soon as he's bored, he'll take off and then too bad for you!"

"How long does it take to get to the beach?" asked the puppet.

"We'll be back within an hour."

"Then, let's run! First one there is the winner!" shouted Pinocchio.

The poor fellow didn't know yet what horrible troubles awaited him.

CHAPTER 27

As soon as he got to the beach, Pinocchio looked out to sea, but he didn't see any Shark.

"Why did you tell me that ridiculous story?" he asked his friends.

"We had our reasons," they answered. "We wanted you to miss school. Serious students like you always make us look bad. You need to quit being so interested in school. If you don't, we'll make you pay."

"You make me laugh," the puppet replied, thrusting out his chin.

"Stop acting so smart and strutting around like a rooster," said the biggest troublemaker. "Don't forget, you're all alone, and there are seven of us."

"Yeah, seven," Pinocchio fired back, "like the seven deadly sins." And he burst out laughing.

"Did you hear that? He insulted us. He called us deadly sins."

"Take it back, Pinocchio. If you don't, you'd better watch out."

"Cuckoo! Here I am," Pinocchio taunted, tapping his nose with his finger to make fun of them.

"I'll give you cuckoo," shouted the strongest boy. And he punched Pinocchio right in the face.

Pinocchio hit back blow for blow, and there was soon a full-scale brawl. Pinocchio kicked with his hard wooden feet. The boys threw their textbooks at his face, first their own books, then Pinocchio's books. One of the boys threw an arithmetic book that weighed a ton at Pinocchio's head, but he missed. The arithmetic book hit another boy instead and knocked him out.

Seeing this, the boys panicked and ran away. Pinocchio alone remained. He called his friend by name and begged him, "Eugene, my poor Eugene! Open your eyes. Look at me! Why don't you say something?"

Then he heard steps approaching.

Two policemen appeared. "What are you doing on the ground?" one of them asked Pinocchio.

"I'm taking care of my friend."

"Did he hurt himself? What happened here?"

Pinocchio picked up the arithmetic book and showed it to the police officers.

"Whose book is this?" asked the police.

"Mine."

"Right. We understand. Get up and follow us."

"But I didn't throw it. . . ."

"Off you go."

Some fishermen were passing, and the police turned over the wounded boy to them. Then they set off down the road with Pinocchio between them. They were just about to the village when a gust of wind blew off Pinocchio's cap and carried it thirty meters away.

"May I go fetch my cap?" Pinocchio asked the police.

"Very well. But be quick."

Pinocchio went to pick up his cap; but instead of putting it on his head, he stuck it between his teeth and set off running as fast as he could toward the beach. Realizing that they wouldn't be able to catch up with him themselves, the police set an enormous Mastiff after him.

CHAPTER 28

Pinocchio is in danger of being fried in a pan like a fish.

As the Dog got closer and closer, Pinocchio thought he was doomed. In fact, Alidor—that was the Dog's name—had almost caught up with Pinocchio. Fortunately they had reached the beach. Pinocchio dived into the waves. Alidor, however, couldn't swim. But he was running so fast he couldn't stop. Alidor ended up in the water too. Exhausted, his eyes filled with terror. "Help! I'm drowning!" the poor Dog begged. "Pinocchio, my friend, save me from death!"

Pinocchio was moved by the heartrending cries. He swam to Alidor, grabbed him by the tail, and tugged him onto the dry sand of the beach. The Dog was too shaken to stand, but even so, Pinocchio was cautious and thought it was wiser to go back into the sea.

"Farewell, Alidor. Good travels and hello to your family."

"Farewell, Pinocchio," answered the Mastiff. "You have done a good deed for me, and in this world a good deed is never lost. If the occasion arises, I'll be as good as my word."

Pinocchio swam on until he arrived in an area that seemed safe to him. There he saw a kind of cave carved into the rocks along the coast. A long plume of smoke streamed from the entrance.

"There must be a fire in this cave," Pinocchio told himself. "So much the better! I can dry off and warm myself. And afterward? Well, we'll see what happens. . . ."

His mind made up, Pinocchio swam toward the rocks. But suddenly he felt something raise him up in the air. He was caught in a big net in the midst of a multitude of fish!

A fisherman as ugly as a sea monster came out of the cave. Imagine his surprise when he found Pinocchio in his net. "What kind of fish is this?" he grumbled. "I have never eaten a fish like this before. It must be some sort of crab."

"What on earth are you talking about?" Pinocchio interrupted. "I'm no crab. Can't you see that I'm a puppet?"

"A puppet?" said the fisherman. "This is the first time I've ever seen a puppet fish! But that's all right. I'll eat you anyway."

"*Eat* me? But I'm trying to tell you that I am not a fish. Don't you hear me talking and reasoning like you?"

Pinocchio wriggled like an eel to escape the grip of the fisherman, so the man tied his ankles and wrists with reeds. Then he rolled him twenty-six times in flour until Pinocchio looked like a plaster puppet. And then the fisherman grabbed him by the head and . . .

CHAPTER 29

Pinocchio returns to the Fairy, who promises him that he will become a real live boy. A party is planned to celebrate the event.

Just as the fisherman was about to toss Pinocchio into the frying pan, a big Dog entered the cave. He moaned softly, wagging his tail as if to say, "Give me some of that fried food and I will leave you alone."

"Save me, Alidor!" Pinocchio whispered. "If you don't, I will be cooked."

The Dog recognized Pinocchio's voice at once. He leaped forward, grabbed the flour-covered puppet, and shot from the cave like a bolt of lightning.

Alidor ran as far as the road that led to the village, then gently set his friend on the ground.

"How can I thank you?" asked Pinocchio.

"Don't worry about it," answered the Mastiff. "You saved my life. A good deed is never wasted." Alidor held out his paw to the puppet, who shook it earnestly. Then they parted.

It was already night when Pinocchio arrived in the village. He went straight to the Fairy's house and tapped the knocker gently. He waited and waited. A good half hour passed before someone opened a window on the top floor of the house and a large Snail with a lighted candle on her head leaned out. "Who is knocking at this hour?"

"Is the Fairy there?" asked Pinocchio.

"The Fairy is sleeping and does not wish to be awakened. But who are you?"

"Pinocchio, the puppet! I live here with the Fairy."

"Very well, I'm coming. Wait for me. I'll be right there."

"For pity's sake, hurry. I'm dying of cold," begged Pinocchio.

"My boy, I do what I can. I am a Snail, and Snails do not go fast."

An hour passed, then two, and still the door didn't open. Losing patience, Pinocchio grabbed the iron door knocker in anger, but it turned into an eel and slipped from his hands. Pinocchio kicked the door with all his strength, so hard that his foot crashed right into the wood. Pinocchio couldn't pull it out. His foot was embedded in the wood like a rivet. He was on the verge of tears, but instead he fainted.

When Pinocchio regained consciousness, he was stretched out on a couch. The Fairy was at his side.

"Again this time I forgive you," she told him. "But woe to you if you get up to your tricks again."

Pinocchio promised that he would study and that from now on he would conduct himself as a good boy should. He gave his word.

"Then tomorrow, Pinocchio, your desire will be met," the Fairy told him. "You will no longer be a wooden puppet. Tomorrow you will become a real child."

Anyone who was not there to see Pinocchio's joy on hearing this great news could not have imagined it! All of his friends were invited to a party the next day to celebrate the event. The Fairy asked for two hundred cups of cappuccino and four hundred slices of buttered bread to be prepared. The next day promised to be marvelous and joyful. But . . .

Unfortunately, in the life of puppets there is always a "but" that spoils everything.

CHAPTER 30

Instead of changing into a little boy, Pinocchio is tempted to sneak off to the Land of Toys with his friend Candlewick.

Of course, Pinocchio immediately asked the Fairy for permission to go out and invite his friends to the party the next day.

"Go ahead," said the Fairy. "But remember, you must return before night. Do you understand?"

"I'll be back in an hour," the puppet assured her.

"Be careful, Pinocchio! Children promise easily, but most of the time they don't keep their word."

"I'm not like other children. When I say something, I do it."

"We will see. But if you disobey, you will regret it."

"Why?"

"Because bad things always happen to children who don't listen to those who know more than they do."

"I've already noticed that," Pinocchio admitted. "But you won't catch me doing it again."

"We'll see if you're telling the truth!"

Pinocchio said good-bye to his good Fairy, who was like a mama to him, and left singing and dancing.

An hour later, he had invited all of his friends, and everyone had accepted except Candlewick, who had not been home. Candlewick was the laziest and wildest boy in the school, but Pinocchio liked him a lot. Where could he find him? He looked everywhere. Finally he found him hidden in a barn under a wagon.

"What are you doing there?" asked Pinocchio.

"I am waiting for midnight to come so I can leave."

"Where are you going?"

"I'm going to live in the Land of Toys. Do you want to come with me?"

"Me? Certainly not!"

"You're making a mistake, Pinocchio! In that wonderful country, vacation begins on the first day of January and ends on the last day of December. Now that's a country that suits me perfectly!"

"What do you do all day in the Land of Toys?" asked the puppet.

"You play. You have fun from morning till evening. In the evening you go to bed, and the next morning you start over. So, are you coming or not?"

"Are you going alone or are others coming?" asked Pinocchio.

"Alone? Why, we'll be in the hundreds! At midnight a wagon will pass by, and it will take us to that extraordinary country. Why don't you come too?" Candlewick asked.

"Don't tempt me. I can't! I promised the Fairy not to go back on my word. So, farewell forever."

"Farewell!" said Candlewick.

Pinocchio thought about it a little more. "When did you say you were leaving?"

"In two hours."

"Too bad! If you were leaving in an hour, I could wait with you."

"But the Fairy?" his friend pointed out.

"I'm already late. One more hour more or less . . ."

"Poor Pinocchio! What if the Fairy scolds you?"

"Too bad! I'll let her talk, and after a while she'll stop."

It was dark when they saw a lantern swinging back and forth in the distance. Soon they heard a soft tinkling of bells and the honk of a horn as high-pitched as the buzz of a mosquito.

"There it is!" Candlewick shouted, jumping up and down.

"What is it?" asked Pinocchio in a hushed voice.

"It's the wagon that's coming to get me. So, are you coming or not?"

"Is it really true that children don't have to go to school in that country?"

"Totally true!"

"What a wonderful country! . . . What a wonderful country! . . . What a wonderful country indeed!"

CHAPTER 31

After five months in the land of delights, Pinocchio gets an unhappy surprise.

At last the wagon arrived—silently, because its wheels were wrapped in burlap and rags. A team of twelve pairs of donkeys pulled the wagon. The coachman was a little man, wider than he was tall, flabby, and as slick and oily as a pat of butter, with a face as red as an apple, lips frozen in a smile, and a soft, caressing voice. The wagon stopped and the little man, smirking, spoke to Candlewick. "Tell me, handsome lad, do you want to go to the land of happiness too?"

"For sure," Candlewick answered. "I want to go."

"And what about you, my good-looking fellow?" asked the coachman.

"I am staying here," said the puppet.

Then Candlewick spoke up. "Listen, Pinocchio. Think of it. We're going to a country where we can do whatever we want from morning to evening."

Pinocchio sighed once, twice, then once more. Finally he said, "All right. Make room for me. "

"The wagon is full," the coachman pointed out, "but to show you how welcome you are, I happily offer you my seat."

"No, no, don't go to such trouble. I will climb on the back of one of these donkeys."

He chose one of the two animals in the lead and jumped onto his back in a single leap. How astonished he was to realize that the little donkey was crying like a child. Frightened, Pinocchio crawled from the donkey's rump to his neck.

"Hey! Ho! Mr. Little Man!" Pinocchio cried out to the wagon driver. "Do you know that this donkey is crying?"

"Come now. We're not going to waste time watching a donkey cry. Sit back where you belong so that we can get started. The night is cold and the journey is long."

Pinocchio obeyed in silence, and the wagon started rolling again. The next morning at dawn they arrived in the Land of Toys.

This country was like no other. In it there lived only children. Bands of kids everywhere playing knucklebones, hopscotch, and ball; riding bicycles and wooden horses; playing blindman's bluff or chasing after each other. Some were singing, others were doing somersaults or walking on their hands. A general wearing a helmet made of leaves was reviewing his papier-mâché troops. Children were laughing, shouting, calling out to one another, clapping their hands, and whistling. The racket was so loud that you'd have to stuff cotton in your ears to keep from going deaf. In every square a tent was set up for a show that crowds of children attended all day long. The walls of houses were covered with charcoal graffiti that said things such as: "Long live toies," "We donn't want skools," "Down with Ari Thematic," and other such gems.

Pinocchio, Candlewick, and all of the children in the little man's wagon plunged into the crowd as soon as they got to town; and as you would guess, they had no trouble making friends with everyone. Impossible to be happier than they were!

Five months passed this way. Day after day they had fun without ever seeing a book or a school. Then one morning Pinocchio awoke to an awful surprise that put him in a dismal mood.

CHAPTER 32

Having first grown long ears and a tail, Pinocchio
begins to bray like a real little donkey.

ᴡhat was this dreadful surprise? When Pinocchio woke, he filled a bowl with water to wash his face, and there he saw something he never wanted to see: his own reflection embellished by a magnificent pair of donkey's ears.

"Oh, poor me! Poor me!" screamed Pinocchio, grabbing his ears and pulling them furiously to rip them off his head.

Hearing his cries, a pretty little Marmot who lived a floor above him entered his room.

"My friend, what are you trying to do?" she asked. "There's nothing you can do about it. It's a scientific fact that all lazy children sooner or later become donkeys. You should have thought about that sooner."

"But it's not my fault! I wanted to be obedient. I wanted to study and do well, but Candlewick told me not to bother with work but instead come with him to the Land of Toys. Oh, if I ever catch him, it will be the worse for him."

He was about to go out, but then he remembered that he had donkey ears. He was ashamed to show himself. So he put on a cotton nightcap and pulled it down to his nose. Then off he went in search of Candlewick, but no one had seen him. Pinocchio went to Candlewick's house and knocked on the door. Finally, after a half hour, Candlewick opened it. Pinocchio couldn't believe what he saw: Candlewick too wore a big cotton nightcap pulled down to his nose!

"Excuse my curiosity, dear Candlewick, but do you happen to have an earache?"

"That's right, Pinocchio. Since this morning I have had an earache."

"And which ear hurts?"

"Both of them. What about you?"

"Both of them. Do you think we have the same sickness?"

"I'm afraid so."

"Would you do something for me, Candlewick, and let me see your ears."

"No problem. But, my dear Pinocchio, I would like to see yours first."

"Let's take off our caps at the same time. Okay? Ready! I will count to three. One! Two! Three!"

At "three" the two boys pulled off their caps and threw them in the air. Instead of being mortified at the sight of their long ears, they burst out laughing. For a long time their sides split with laughter; but suddenly Candlewick stopped, turned pale, and staggered. "Help, Pinocchio!" he called out. "Help me! My legs won't support me anymore."

"Mine neither!" cried Pinocchio. Tottering, he burst into tears.

Their legs folded beneath them, and they dropped to the floor on their hands and knees. Their hands changed into hooves, their faces grew longer and turned into muzzles, and their backs were covered in light gray hair with black spots. But the very worst moment, the very worst humiliation, was when they each felt a tail growing. Overcome by shame and sadness, they tried to complain and wail, but the only sound they could make was "Hee-haw! Hee-haw! Hee-haw!"

Just then someone knocked on the door and commanded, "Open up! I am the little man, the wagon driver, who brought you here. Open immediately or else!"

CHAPTER 33

Having become a real donkey, Pinocchio is sold to a circus manager, who teaches him to dance and leap in circles. One evening he injures himself and is sold for his hide.

When the door remained closed, the little man kicked it open and entered the room. "Bravo, boys!" he said, smiling insincerely. "Your braying is perfect. I recognized you at once. In fact, that's why I came."

Then he put halters on them and led them to the market in the hope of selling them for a good price. And, in fact, buyers weren't long in showing up. Candlewick was bought by a farmer who had lost his donkey the day before and Pinocchio by the manager of a circus.

After leading him to the stable, Pinocchio's new master filled his manger with straw. Pinocchio tasted it then spit it out. "Hee-haw! Hee-haw! I can't digest this straw."

"Do you think I bought you in order to give you food and water?" shouted the manager. "I bought you to work and make me lots of money. On your feet, let's go. You're coming with me to the circus ring where I'll teach you how to leap in circles and dance the waltz and polka standing on your hind legs."

And that is what happened. Poor Pinocchio had to learn to do all those things whether he liked it or not; but it took him three months to learn, and he got lots of lashes with the whip.

One day his master finally announced an extraordinary spectacle on signs posted on every street corner:

APPEARING TONIGHT
A GRAND GALA SPECTACLE
of acrobatics and surprising feats
by all the artists and horses of the Company—
AND, for the first time, the famous
LITTLE DONKEY PINOCCHIO,
the Star of the Dance

Of course, the theater was packed on this memorable evening. The bleachers were filled with children of all ages, excited at the idea of seeing the famous donkey Pinocchio dance. There was thunderous applause when Pinocchio entered the ring. Two white camellias decorated his ears, his braided mane was sprinkled with silver, and velvet ribbons were wrapped around his tail.

"Go, Pinocchio! Show these ladies and gentlemen how elegantly you can leap."

Pinocchio made several tries, but each time he approached the hoop, he went under it instead of through it. He gathered his forces for another try, and this time he almost succeeded. But his hind legs got caught in the hoop, and he fell in a heap on the ground. When he got up again, he limped. He had the greatest difficulty returning to the stable.

"Pinocchio, come back! We want the donkey! Pinocchio! Pinocchio!" roared the children, moved by what they had seen.

But the donkey didn't return. The next morning the veterinarian declared that Pinocchio would be lame for the rest of his life. So the circus manager called the stable boy. "What am I supposed to do with a lame donkey? Take him to the market and sell him."

At the market they immediately found a buyer.

"How much for this lame donkey?"

"Twenty lire."

"I'll give you twenty centesimi. After all, I'm not going to use him. I'm buying him only for his hide. I need it to make myself a drum for the village orchestra."

I leave it to you, children, to imagine Pinocchio's feelings when he heard that he was going to become a drum!

After paying the twenty centesimi, the buyer led the donkey to a rock by the sea and tied a heavy stone around his neck. Fastening a rope to one leg, he held the other end in his hand and shoved Pinocchio into the water. Then the man sat on the boulder and waited for the donkey to drown so that he could recover his hide.

CHAPTER 34

The donkey Pinocchio becomes a puppet again. While swimming for his life, he is swallowed by a terrible Shark.

The donkey was in the water for almost an hour.

"He should be completely drowned by now," the man said to himself. He pulled on the rope, but instead of a dead donkey, he pulled up a puppet, very much alive and wriggling like an eel.

"And the donkey I threw into the sea, where is he?" asked the man.

"The donkey is me!" The puppet laughed.

"But how did you become a wooden puppet?"

"No doubt from the effects of salt water."

"Enough, puppet! Don't expect to laugh at my expense. I paid twenty centesimi for you, and I want my money back. I'm taking you back to the market to sell as firewood."

"Okay, sell me again! I would be delighted," replied Pinocchio, and he leaped back into the sea and swam away as fast as he could. Soon he was no more than a little black dot on the surface of the water.

Swimming along haphazardly, Pinocchio saw a craggy white rock on which a pretty little Goat stood bleating. Her coat was a striking blue like the hair of the Fairy. Doubling his effort, Pinocchio turned toward her just as a huge horrible head broke the surface—a sea monster was coming to meet him. His wide-open mouth was like a cavern, revealing three rows of teeth!

"Hurry, Pinocchio! I beg you!" bleated the little Goat.

But it was too late! The monster caught up with Pinocchio and swallowed the poor puppet the way you might gulp down an egg. Inside the Shark, Pinocchio tumbled about so violently that he lost consciousness for a good fifteen minutes.

When he came to, he was in the blackest darkness. Pinocchio tried to keep up his courage, but when he finally understood that he was truly inside the monster, he collapsed in tears.

"Help! Help! Is there no one who can save me?"

"Who could save you, poor fellow?" said a scratchy voice in the darkness.

"Who's talking?" asked Pinocchio, trembling with fear.

"Me. I'm a poor Tuna Fish that the Shark has also swallowed."

While they talked, Pinocchio thought he saw a dim light in the distance. "That light over there, what is it?" he asked.

"No doubt it is another poor being who is waiting to be digested."

"I'm going to see. Maybe it's an old fish who knows how to get out of here. Farewell, Tuna!"

"Farewell, and good luck!" answered the Tuna.

CHAPTER 35

Pinocchio finds someone in the belly of the Shark.
Who is it? Read this chapter and find out.

Pinocchio groped his way one step at a time through the darkness inside the Shark toward the faint light in the distance. As he moved forward, the light grew brighter until at last he reached it—and what did he find? I'll give you a thousand guesses.

There before him was a little table and on it a glowing candle stuck in a green glass bottle. Sitting at the table was a little old man.

Pinocchio was delirious with happiness. He wanted to laugh and cry at the same time. Finally, he shouted with joy and ran to embrace the old man.

"Oh, my dear papa! At last I have found you. I will never ever leave you again. Never!"

The old man rubbed his eyes. "Then what I am seeing is real? You are truly my dear Pinocchio?"

"I am really and truly Pinocchio! And you have forgiven me, haven't you? My dear papa, you are so good . . . while I, to think that I . . . Oh, if you only knew the misfortunes that have befallen me. It all started that day that you, my dear papa, sold your coat to buy me a spelling book so I could go to school and instead I ran away to see a puppet show."

Pinocchio told his papa everything that had happened to him: how the puppet master was going to use him as firewood to roast a sheep but instead gave him five gold coins; how he met the Fox and the Cat and was hung from a tree and then saved by the beautiful Blue-Haired Fairy; how he told a lie and his nose grew longer; how he stole grapes and had to serve as a watchdog; and how he returned to the home of the Fairy to find that she had died.

Pinocchio continued his story. "Then a Pigeon flew me on his back to the seashore where I saw you in a boat on the sea and I waved at you to come back."

"I recognized you and wanted to come back," said Geppetto, "but the sea was heaving and a huge wave capsized my boat. A terrible Shark saw me in the water and swallowed me whole. It's been two years since then—two years that have seemed like centuries!"

"How did you stay alive? Where did you get the candle and matches?"

"Here is what happened. A merchant ship went down in the same storm. The sailors were saved but the ship sank to the bottom, and along came the hungry Shark. After he had swallowed me, he swallowed the ship. I have lived off the ship's cargo for two years: tinned meat, biscuits, wine, raisins, cheese, coffee, and sugar. But the supplies have run out now—nothing is left except this candle, and when it burns out, we shall be in the dark."

"Then, dear little Papa, we must escape out of the mouth of the Shark and into the sea. There is no time to lose."

"But I don't know how to swim."

"I'm a good swimmer. I'll carry you on my shoulders and swim to shore." Pinocchio took the candle and led the way. "Follow me. And don't be afraid."

It took a long time for them to walk through the Shark's body. When they reached the point where the throat began, they stopped to determine the best moment to escape.

Before I continue, I must tell you that the Shark was old and suffered from asthma and heart palpitations and had to sleep with his mouth open. So when Pinocchio reached the end of the Shark's throat, he could look out the enormous, gaping mouth and see a section of starry sky and beautiful moonlight.

"Now is the moment to escape," Pinocchio whispered to his father. "The Shark is sleeping like a dormouse, the sea is calm, and it's as light as day out there. Follow me, dear Papa, and we will soon be safe."

They climbed up the Shark's throat and tiptoed down his tongue. Before taking a final leap, Pinocchio told his father, "Climb onto my back and wrap your arms tightly around my neck. I will do the rest."

With Geppetto settled on his shoulders, Pinocchio jumped into the water and started swimming. The sea was as smooth as glass, the moon shone brightly, and the Shark slept so soundly that a cannon blast could not have roused him.

CHAPTER 36

At last Pinocchio stops being a puppet and becomes a boy.

While Pinocchio swam toward shore with his father clinging to his neck, his strength began to fail him. He swam until he ran out of breath. Then he gasped. "Papa . . . help me. . . . I am dying!"

"Who is dying?" asked a voice that sounded like an out-of-tune guitar.

"Me and my poor father!"

"I recognize that voice. Pinocchio!"

"You are right. And you?"

"I am the Tuna Fish you met when we were imprisoned in the Shark's body. You showed me the way out. I followed you and escaped after you."

"You have arrived just in time. Help us or we will die."

"Both of you, climb on my back, and I will take you to shore."

In no time at all, Pinocchio jumped onto the beach, then helped his father. He thanked the Tuna Fish with heartfelt sincerity, and when the Tuna poked his head out of the water, Pinocchio kissed him on the nose. The fish quickly plunged back into the sea for fear that he would be seen crying at the puppet's gesture of affection and gratitude.

"Lean on me, dear Papa, and we will search for a house or cottage where someone will kindly give us a mouthful of bread and a little straw for a bed."

After a short while they came upon two scruffy-looking beggars by the side of the road. Scarcely recognizable, they were the Cat and the Fox. The Cat had feigned blindness for so long that she had become blind; and the Fox, now old, mangy, and paralyzed on one side, no longer had a tail. Because he was so poor, he had sold his beautiful tail to a peddler, who bought it to shoo away flies.

"Oh, Pinocchio, a little charity for two sick people," cried the Fox.

"Farewell, impostors!" answered the puppet. "You fooled me once, but you won't do it again."

Soon Pinocchio and Geppetto came to a path that led to a little straw hut in the middle of a field. They went to the door and knocked.

"Turn the key," said a little voice, "and the door will open."

This is just what Pinocchio did. Then they went in and looked everywhere, but they couldn't find anyone.

"Where is the master of the house?" said Pinocchio.

"Here I am—up here."

Looking up, Pinocchio and his father saw the Talking Cricket sitting on a beam near the ceiling.

"Oh, my dear little Cricket!" said Pinocchio, bowing politely.

"Now you call me 'my dear little Cricket.' Do you remember when you threw a hammer handle at me to chase me away?'"

"It's true, Cricket. I did. Throw a hammer handle at me then, but have pity on my poor papa."

"I will have pity on both of you, but I wanted to remind you of the way you ill-used me. I wanted to teach you that in this world, it is better to be courteous to others if you wish to receive courtesy in your hour of need."

"You're right, Cricket, and I will remember your lesson. But tell me, how were you able to buy this charming hut."

"The hut was given to me yesterday by a Goat with beautiful blue wool."

"And where has the Goat gone?" asked Pinocchio.

"I don't know."

"And when will it come back?"

"Never. It went away yesterday grieving and bleating in a way that seemed to say, 'Poor Pinocchio . . . I shall never see him again. . . . The Shark has eaten him!"

"Did it really say that? Then it was her! My dear little Fairy!" shouted Pinocchio, and he began to sob.

He wept for some time. Then he dried his eyes and prepared a comfortable bed of straw for Geppetto. "Tell me, little Cricket," he asked, "where can I find a glass of milk for my poor papa?"

"You will find milk at Giangio the farmer's, three fields away."

Pinocchio ran to Giangio's house.

"A glass of milk will cost you a halfpenny," said the farmer.

"I don't have any money at all," replied Pinocchio sadly.

"I'm sure we can come to an agreement. Will you turn the pumping machine? If you draw up a hundred buckets of water from the well, I'll give you a glass of milk."

Pinocchio set to work immediately, but before he had drawn up the hundred buckets, sweat poured from his head to his feet. Never had he worked so hard.

"Up until now," the farmer said, "my little Donkey turned the machine, but the poor animal is dying."

"Will you take me to him?" Pinocchio asked.

When Pinocchio went into the stable, he saw a beautiful little Donkey stretched out on the straw, hungry and worn-out from overwork. As he looked at the Donkey, Pinocchio felt disturbed. "I know this little Donkey."

The little Donkey opened his dying eyes and said weakly, "I am . . . Can . . . dle . . . wick . . . ," and then he died.

"Poor Candlewick," Pinocchio murmured, and took a handful of straw to dry a tear streaming down his cheek.

For five months Pinocchio rose each day before dawn and turned the pumping machine to earn the milk that was so good for his father. Not content with that job alone, he used his free time to make hampers and baskets from rushes. Thanks to the money he earned in this way, he was able to take care of his ailing father. He even managed to save enough to buy himself a new jacket.

"I'm going to the market to buy myself a jacket, a cap, and a pair of shoes," Pinocchio told Geppetto one day. "When I come back, I will be so finely dressed that you will take me for a gentleman."

He left the house and was running happily along when he heard someone call his name. A large Snail was crawling out from underneath a hedge.

"Do you remember me?" she asked. "The Snail who was maid to the Fairy? Don't you remember when I came downstairs to let you in and your foot was stuck in the front door?"

"I remember!" shouted Pinocchio. "Tell me now, where is my good Fairy? What is she doing? Has she forgiven me? Is she far away? Can I go see her?"

"My dear Pinocchio, the poor Fairy is gravely ill and doesn't have enough money to buy even a crust of bread."

"Oh, my poor Fairy! If I had money, I would give it all to her, but I have only forty centesimi. I was going to buy a new jacket, but you take these coins, Snail. Take them to my good Fairy."

"And your new jacket?"

"It doesn't matter. I would sell the rags off my back to help her. Go, Snail. Hurry. In two days I'll come back to this place and bring you more money. I have been working to take care of my papa. Today I will work five hours more so that I can take care of my good mama."

That night Pinocchio stayed up late and made sixteen baskets instead of eight. He finally went to bed, and while he slept, he dreamed that the Fairy came to him and kissed him.

"Well done, Pinocchio! Because of your good heart I will forgive you. Boys who take care of their parents and help them when they are old and suffering deserve praise and affection, even if they have not been obedient and good. Try to do better in the future and you will be happy."

Imagine Pinocchio's surprise when he awoke and discovered that he was no longer a wooden puppet but instead had become a real live boy. When he looked around, he saw that he was no longer in a straw hut but instead in a nice little room furnished with elegant simplicity. He got out of bed and put on the new suit of clothes that was laid out for him with a new cap and leather boots that fit him perfectly.

He reached into his pocket and pulled out a coin purse on which was written: "The Blue-Haired Fairy wishes to return the forty coins to her dear Pinocchio and thank him for his good heart."

But when Pinocchio opened the purse, instead of forty copper pennies, he found forty shiny gold coins.

When he looked in the mirror, he was bewildered. He didn't see the wooden puppet he had always seen before. Instead he was greeted by the joyful face of a bright boy with brown hair and blue eyes.

"Where is Papa?" he shouted, and ran into the next room. There was old Geppetto well again and happily plying his trade. He was carving leaves and flowers and animals into a beautiful wooden frame.

Pinocchio hugged his father. "How could this have happened?" he asked.

"All because of you," answered Geppetto. "When boys who behave badly turn over a new leaf and become good, they have the power to bring contentment and happiness to their families."

"Where is the old wooden Pinocchio now?"

Geppetto pointed to a big puppet propped against a chair with its head drooping to one side, its arms dangling, and its legs crossed in such a way that it was amazing it could ever stand.

Pinocchio stood staring at the puppet for a little while. Then, with great satisfaction, he said to himself, "How ridiculous I was when I was a puppet! And how happy I am to have become a real boy."

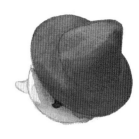

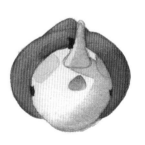